Silly Mummy, Silly Daddy

Marie-Louise Fitzpatrick

F

FRANCES LINCOLN
CHILDREN'S BOOKS

Beth won't smile today.

Silly Mummy.

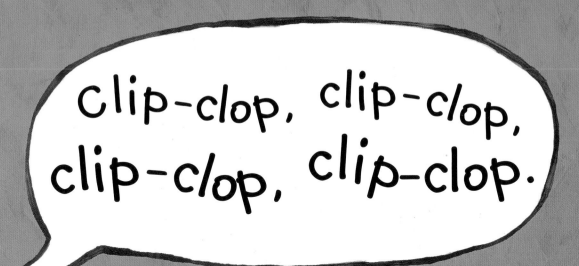

Silly Daddy.

Silly Granny.

Silly Grandad.

Silly Aunty Bea.

Silly Uncle Ben.

Silly Aunty Mel.

Sillybillies.

Here comes Ann.

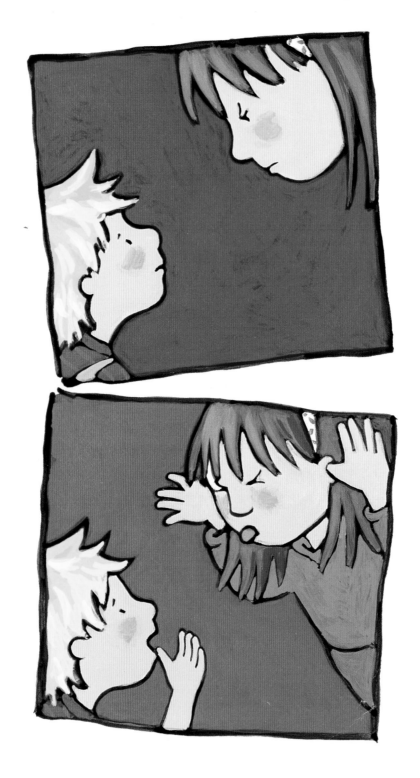

Clever big sister!